The Net Effect

How the Internet Transformed Our World

Asif Ahmed Srabon

ISBN 978-93-5883-120-7
© Asif Ahmed Srabon 2023

Published in India 2023 by Pencil

Contributors:
Editor: Asif Ahmed Srabon

A brand of
One Point Six Technologies Pvt. Ltd.
Unit no. 26, Ground Floor, Building A1,
Wadala Truck Terminal Road,
Near Post Office, Antop Hill, Mumbai - 400037
E connect@thepencilapp.com
W www.thepencilapp.com

Author biography

Asif Ahmed Srabon, an enigmatic figure in the world of American literature, was born on July 4, 2003, in the vibrant city of Philadelphia, Pennsylvania, USA. A prolific writer, Asif has captivated readers with his profound insights into American history and culture. Despite his literary accomplishments, he remains fiercely private about his education and academic qualifications, leaving an air of mystery surrounding his early life. This biography delves into the life and works of Asif Ahmed Srabon, a master storyteller who has left an indelible mark on the literary landscape.

Early Life:

Asif Ahmed Srabon was born to a close-knit family in the heart of Philadelphia. Little is known about his upbringing and formative years, as he seldom speaks about his personal life. From an early age, he exhibited an insatiable appetite for reading, which later evolved into a passion for writing. Asif's curiosity about history and its connection to contemporary society became evident through his musings, even during his youth.

Literary Journey:

Asif's literary journey began in his teenage years, where he discovered his talent for crafting narratives that captured the essence of America's past. He started writing short stories and essays, which demonstrated a remarkable ability to engage readers with his compelling prose. Despite his youth, Asif displayed a maturity in his writing that belied his age, leaving readers curious about the mind behind these words.

In the Shadows:

Asif Ahmed Srabon remained a reclusive figure throughout his writing career, shying away from public appearances and interviews. He preferred to let his words speak for themselves, refusing to disclose details about his education and academic qualifications. This choice further heightened the intrigue surrounding his persona and allowed readers to interpret his works in their unique ways, unburdened by the writer's personal background.

Publication of "America: From Revolution to the Present Day":

In a moment that defined Asif's literary legacy, he published his seminal work, "America: From Revolution to the Present Day." This ambitious undertaking sought to explore the multifaceted history of the United States, weaving together historical events, cultural nuances, and societal transformations into a comprehensive narrative. The book received critical acclaim for its captivating storytelling and profound analysis, solidifying Asif's place as a significant voice in American literature.

Philosophy and Themes:

Asif Ahmed Srabon's writings often delved into themes of identity, social justice, and the interconnectedness of history. Through his prose, he invited readers to confront the complexities of the American experience and to reflect on the nation's triumphs and shortcomings. His narratives often provided insights into marginalized voices, shedding light on forgotten aspects of history that deserved attention and contemplation.

Legacy:

Asif Ahmed Srabon's works continue to resonate with readers across the globe. He remains a literary enigma, challenging conventional norms by separating his writing from the persona behind it. Through his profound narratives and poignant exploration of America's past, Asif has left an enduring legacy that invites readers to question, to learn, and to empathize.

Conclusion:

Asif Ahmed Srabon, born on the Fourth of July, emerged as a compelling figure in American literature. Despite his privacy regarding his personal life and academic background, his writings have transcended barriers and captured the hearts and minds of countless readers. Through his literary prowess, Asif has become a powerful storyteller, illuminating the diverse tapestry of America's history and inspiring future generations of writers to explore the depth of human experiences through the written word. The enigma of Asif Ahmed Srabon will forever intrigue, and his contributions to literature will stand the test of time.

CONTENTS

History of the Internet

The internet's origin can be traced back to the early 1960s when the United States Department of Defense's Advanced Research Projects Agency (ARPA) envisioned a decentralized communication system that could maintain communication in the event of a nuclear attack. This led to the development of the ARPANET, which became the foundation of the modern internet.

In 1969, the first successful message was transmitted over the ARPANET between computers at the University of California, Los Angeles (UCLA) and the Stanford Research Institute (SRI). This marked the birth of the internet as we know it today. Throughout the 1970s, more institutions and research centers joined the ARPANET, expanding its reach.

In 1983, the ARPANET adopted the TCP/IP protocol, a set of rules that allowed different networks to communicate with each other. This standardization paved the way for the internet to become a global network of interconnected computers.

In the late 1980s and early 1990s, the National Science Foundation (NSF) in the United States played a crucial role in developing the internet further. They funded the creation of a high-speed backbone network called NSFNET, which connected various supercomputer centers and universities. This backbone significantly increased the speed and capacity of the internet.

In 1991, the World Wide Web (WWW) was introduced by British computer scientist Tim Berners-Lee. He developed the Hypertext Transfer Protocol (HTTP) and the Hypertext Markup Language (HTML), allowing users to access and share information in a user-friendly way through web browsers. This revolutionized the internet and made it accessible to a broader audience.

As the internet's popularity grew, commercial interests began to recognize its potential. In the mid-1990s, internet service providers (ISPs) emerged, offering access to the internet for individual users. The development of web browsers like Netscape Navigator and Internet Explorer further accelerated the internet's expansion.

The early 2000s witnessed the rise of e-commerce, social media, and search engines, further transforming the internet into an integral part of daily life for billions of people worldwide. Innovations like Google, Facebook, YouTube, and Twitter reshaped how we access information, communicate, and share content.

The evolution of mobile devices and the widespread adoption of smartphones in the late 2000s brought the internet to even more people, enabling access on the go.

In recent years, the internet has continued to evolve with the emergence of cloud computing, artificial intelligence, Internet of Things (IoT), and other technological advancements, opening up new possibilities and challenges for our connected world.

Today, the internet plays an indispensable role in various aspects of modern society, from communication and entertainment to business, education, and research. Its history is a testament to human ingenuity and collaboration, and it continues to shape the world in ways that were once unimaginable.

The invention of the Internet and its use

The invention of the internet can be traced back to the late 1960s, with the development of the ARPANET (Advanced Research Projects Agency Network) by the United States Department of Defense's Advanced Research Projects Agency (ARPA). The primary goal of ARPANET was to create a decentralized communication network that could withstand partial destruction due to a nuclear attack.

In 1969, the first successful message transmission over ARPANET occurred between two universities in California - Stanford and UCLA. This event marked the birth of the internet as we know it today. Over the next few decades, the network expanded to include more research institutions and government agencies, facilitating the exchange of information and research findings.

The internet continued to evolve in the 1980s and 1990s, with the development of TCP/IP (Transmission Control Protocol/Internet Protocol) as the standard communication protocol for interconnecting networks. This advancement made it possible for various networks to communicate with each other, leading to the creation of a vast global network of interconnected computers.

The World Wide Web (WWW) was another crucial milestone in the history of the internet. In 1989, British computer scientist Sir Tim Berners-Lee proposed the concept of the WWW while working at CERN, the European Organization for Nuclear Research. He created the first web browser and server and introduced the idea of hypertext, allowing users to access information by clicking on hyperlinks. This breakthrough made the internet more accessible and user-friendly, leading to its widespread adoption and popularity.

As the internet became more accessible to the public in the 1990s, its uses expanded rapidly. Today, the internet has become an integral part of our daily lives, revolutionizing communication, commerce, education, and much more. Some of the past and present uses of the internet include:

Communication: Email, instant messaging, and social media platforms have transformed the way we communicate, allowing real-time interactions with people across the globe.

Information Access: The internet provides a vast repository of information on virtually any topic, accessible through search engines, online libraries, and databases.

E-Commerce: Online shopping has become a norm, enabling consumers to purchase goods and services from the comfort of their homes.

Social Networking: Social media platforms like Facebook, Twitter, and Instagram have revolutionized how we connect and share information with others.

Education: Online courses and e-learning platforms have made education more accessible and convenient, allowing people to learn at their own pace from anywhere.

Entertainment: Streaming services for movies, TV shows, music, and gaming have become incredibly popular, transforming the way we consume entertainment content.

Business and Collaboration: The internet has enabled businesses to operate globally, connect with clients, and collaborate with teams in different parts of the world.

Research and Innovation: Scientists and researchers can collaborate, share findings, and access vast amounts of data, accelerating the pace of innovation and discovery.

Healthcare: Telemedicine and online health resources have facilitated remote consultations and improved access to medical information.

News and Media: The internet has revolutionized journalism, allowing news to be delivered instantly and enabling citizen journalism.

While the internet has brought about numerous advancements and conveniences, it also poses challenges such as cybersecurity threats, privacy concerns, and the digital divide. As technology continues to evolve, the internet will undoubtedly play an even more significant role in shaping the future of society and communications.

Different branches of the Internet

World Wide Web (WWW): The web of interconnected pages and content accessible through web browsers.

Email: Electronic mail for sending and receiving messages over the Internet.

File Transfer Protocol (FTP): Used for uploading and downloading files between computers.

Instant Messaging: Real-time communication through text messages.

Social Media: Platforms for sharing content and connecting with others online.

Online Gaming: Video games played over the Internet with other players.

E-commerce: Online shopping and business transactions conducted over the Internet.

Search Engines: Tools used to search for information on the web.

Cloud Computing: Accessing and storing data and software through remote servers.

Video Streaming: Delivering video content over the Internet in real-time.

These are just a few examples of the many branches that make up the vast and interconnected world of the Internet.

How the Internet Works

The internet is a vast global network of interconnected computers and servers that allows the exchange of data and information. Its functionality relies on several key components and protocols:

Devices: At the core of the internet are various devices, such as computers, smartphones, tablets, servers, routers, and switches. These devices are connected through various technologies like Ethernet, Wi-Fi, and cellular networks.

IP Addresses: Every device on the internet is assigned a unique identifier called an IP (Internet Protocol) address. This address helps in identifying the source and destination of data packets during communication.

Data Packets: Data is transmitted over the internet in small units called data packets. Each packet contains the sender's and receiver's IP addresses, data content, and other information necessary for routing.

Routers: Routers are essential networking devices that forward data packets between different networks. They act as traffic directors, determining the best path for data to reach its destination.

Protocols: The internet relies on several communication protocols to ensure data transmission is standardized and efficient. The two main protocols are TCP (Transmission Control Protocol) and IP (Internet Protocol). TCP establishes a reliable connection between devices, while IP handles the addressing and routing of data packets.

DNS (Domain Name System): The DNS is like the internet's phone book, translating human-readable domain names (e.g., www.example.com) into IP addresses. This conversion enables users to access websites without remembering long strings of numbers.

HTTP (Hypertext Transfer Protocol): HTTP is a protocol used for transmitting web pages and other content over the internet. It governs how web browsers and servers communicate, enabling users to browse websites and access resources.

HTTPS (Hypertext Transfer Protocol Secure): HTTPS is a secure version of HTTP that encrypts data during transmission, ensuring privacy and protection against potential eavesdropping or tampering.

Firewalls and Security Measures: Firewalls are network security devices that monitor and control incoming and outgoing traffic, protecting networks from unauthorized access and potential threats.

Internet Service Providers (ISPs): ISPs are companies that provide users with access to the internet. They act as intermediaries between users and the vast network of servers and websites.

When you send a request to access a website, your device initiates a series of interactions with servers through data packets. Routers guide these packets along the most efficient path until they reach the destination server. The server processes the request and sends back the requested data, which is again broken down into packets and routed back to your device, where it is reassembled and displayed on your screen.

This process happens within milliseconds and is repeated countless times each day as billions of devices communicate, ensuring the internet's seamless functionality that we rely on for information, communication, and entertainment.

Advantages and disadvantages of the internet

Advantages of the Internet:

Information Access: The internet provides instant access to a vast amount of information on almost any topic. It allows users to gather knowledge, conduct research, and stay updated on current events from around the world.

Communication: The internet enables seamless and instantaneous communication through various platforms such as email, social media, video conferencing, and messaging apps, connecting people across the globe.

Global Connectivity: It breaks down geographical barriers and fosters global connections, facilitating international collaborations, business partnerships, and cultural exchange.

E-commerce: The internet revolutionized commerce, enabling online shopping and digital transactions, making it convenient for consumers and businesses alike.

Education and E-Learning: E-learning platforms and online educational resources have expanded educational opportunities, making learning accessible to people of all ages and backgrounds.

Entertainment: The internet offers a plethora of entertainment options, including streaming services, online gaming, social media content, and creative platforms.

Job Opportunities: It has created numerous job opportunities in fields like digital marketing, content creation, web development, and more.

Social Networking: The internet allows people to connect and interact with friends, family, and like-minded individuals through social networking sites, fostering virtual communities.

Innovation and Collaboration: The internet has facilitated collaboration among researchers, innovators, and professionals across diverse industries, leading to technological advancements.

Government Services: Many governments provide online services, such as e-filing of taxes, online bill payments, and access to official documents, making interactions with authorities more convenient.

Disadvantages of the Internet:

Information Overload: The abundance of information on the internet can be overwhelming, leading to difficulties in discerning accurate and reliable sources from misleading or false ones.

Privacy Concerns: The internet poses risks to personal privacy, as users' data can be collected, tracked, and misused by malicious entities or for targeted advertising purposes.

Cybersecurity Threats: The internet is susceptible to cyber attacks, including hacking, data breaches, phishing scams, and malware infections, which can compromise individuals and organizations.

Addiction and Distractions: Excessive internet usage can lead to addiction and adversely impact productivity, relationships, and mental health.

Spread of Misinformation: The ease of sharing information on the internet can lead to the rapid spread of misinformation and fake news, potentially influencing public opinion and decision-making.

Social Isolation: Excessive reliance on online communication can lead to reduced face-to-face interactions, contributing to feelings of isolation and loneliness.

Digital Divide: Not everyone has equal access to the internet, creating a digital divide between those with reliable internet access and those without, leading to unequal opportunities.

Online Harassment and Cyberbullying: The anonymity of the internet can embolden individuals to engage in harmful behavior, such as cyberbullying and online harassment.

Copyright Infringement: The ease of copying and sharing digital content has led to copyright violations and piracy issues, impacting artists, authors, and content creators.

Health Concerns: Prolonged screen time and sedentary internet usage can lead to various health problems, including eye strain, sleep disturbances, and posture-related issues.

In conclusion, while the internet has brought about significant advancements and positive changes in various aspects of life, it also comes with its fair share of challenges and drawbacks that society must address and mitigate. Responsible usage, awareness of potential risks, and implementing robust cybersecurity measures are crucial for harnessing the internet's benefits while minimizing its disadvantages.

Benefits of people through internet

Once upon a time, in the not-so-distant past, the world witnessed a technological revolution that transformed society in ways unimaginable. This transformation came in the form of the internet, a vast network connecting people, information, and ideas from every corner of the globe.

As the internet grew in popularity, it became a powerful tool that revolutionized various aspects of human life. One of the most significant areas of impact was communication. Long gone were the days of waiting weeks for a letter to arrive; now, instant messaging and video calls allowed people to connect with loved ones and friends across continents, bridging distances and time zones effortlessly. Families could share experiences, celebrate milestones, and stay in touch, strengthening their bonds regardless of physical separation.

In the realm of education, the internet opened up new horizons for learning. Online courses and virtual classrooms made education accessible to anyone with an internet connection, transcending geographical barriers and financial limitations. People could now pursue degrees, acquire new skills, and enhance their knowledge without leaving their homes. Knowledge became democratized, empowering individuals to seek personal and professional growth on their terms.

The internet also revolutionized commerce, giving rise to the era of e-commerce. Online marketplaces provided a platform for entrepreneurs and small businesses to reach a global customer base. Customers enjoyed the convenience of shopping from the comfort of their homes, comparing prices, and accessing a vast array of products and services with just a few clicks. This digital marketplace not only boosted the economy but also offered opportunities for innovative startups to thrive.

Additionally, the internet empowered creatives and content creators. Social media platforms became avenues for sharing art, music, photography, and writing, allowing talented individuals to showcase their work to a wide audience. As a result, artists could gain recognition, collaborate with like-minded individuals, and turn their passions into sustainable careers.

The internet even revolutionized healthcare. Telemedicine emerged as a game-changer, enabling remote consultations and medical services. Patients in rural areas or with limited mobility found it easier to access medical expertise, while medical professionals could collaborate and share knowledge with colleagues worldwide, fostering advancements in the field of medicine.

In the realm of information dissemination, the internet became a treasure trove of knowledge. Online libraries, databases, and search engines empowered individuals to access vast amounts of information, making research and self-learning more efficient than ever before. People could now stay updated on current events, access scientific research, and explore different perspectives on a wide range of topics.

Environmental consciousness also benefited from the internet. Virtual meetings and remote work options reduced the need for extensive travel, leading to lower carbon emissions and a positive impact on the environment. People found ways to share eco-friendly practices, fostering a global movement towards sustainability.

In conclusion, the internet's incredible reach and accessibility have revolutionized the way people interact, learn, work, create, and access information. It has broken down barriers, enriched lives, and connected humanity like never before. As technology continues to evolve, the internet's potential for positive impact on society remains boundless, promising a brighter future for generations to come.

YouTube

YouTube is a video-sharing platform that was founded on February 14, 2005, by three former PayPal employees: Chad Hurley, Steve Chen, and Jawed Karim. The website was officially launched to the public in November 2005 and quickly became a global phenomenon. It allows users to upload, share, and view videos on a wide range of topics, making it one of the most popular and influential websites on the internet.

Key Features and Functionality:

Video Uploads: Users can upload videos to their own channels, and the platform supports a variety of video formats and resolutions.

Channel Creation: Anyone with a Google account can create a YouTube channel to share their content with the world. Channels can be personalized with custom banners, profile pictures, and descriptions.

Viewing and Subscribing: Users can watch videos from other creators and subscribe to their channels to receive notifications when new content is uploaded.

Likes, Dislikes, and Comments: Viewers can express their opinion on videos by giving them a thumbs-up (like) or thumbs-down (dislike). They can also leave comments to engage with the creator and other viewers.

Monetization: YouTube offers various monetization options for creators to earn revenue from their content. The YouTube Partner Program (YPP) enables creators to earn money through ads, channel memberships, and merchandise shelf features.

YouTube Premium: Users can subscribe to YouTube Premium to enjoy an ad-free experience, offline downloads, and access to YouTube Originals.

Content and Categories:
YouTube hosts an immense variety of content, catering to a broad range of interests and niches. Some common content categories include:

Entertainment: Music videos, movie trailers, web series, and comedy sketches.
Educational: Tutorials, documentaries, how-to guides, and academic lectures.
Gaming: Gameplay videos, reviews, and live streams.
Vlogging: Personal vlogs, travel diaries, and daily life updates.
DIY and Crafts: Instructional videos for creative projects.
Health and Fitness: Workouts, wellness tips, and healthy recipes.
Challenges and Controversies:

Over the years, YouTube has faced several challenges and controversies:

Copyright Infringement: The platform has had to deal with copyright violations due to the unauthorized use of copyrighted content in videos.

Content Moderation: Ensuring appropriate content and handling controversial material have been ongoing challenges for YouTube, as it strives to maintain a balance between free speech and responsible content management.

Advertiser Boycotts: There have been instances when major advertisers suspended their campaigns on YouTube due to concerns about their ads appearing next to inappropriate or extremist content.

Community Guidelines: YouTube has had to refine and enforce its community guidelines to combat harmful and inappropriate content, such as hate speech, harassment, and misinformation.

Children's Content: YouTube faced scrutiny for content targeted at children and concerns about child safety, leading to changes in the platform's policies and features.

Popularity and Impact:
YouTube's impact on popular culture and online communication is undeniable. It has given rise to countless internet celebrities and content creators, providing a platform for creative expression and knowledge-sharing.

The site has played a significant role in shaping entertainment trends, music discovery, and the democratization of media.

With billions of users and millions of hours of video content uploaded every day, YouTube remains a dominant force in the digital landscape, connecting people from all over the world through videos. It continues to evolve and adapt, influencing how we consume media and interact with online communities.

Facebook

Facebook is a social media platform founded by Mark Zuckerberg, along with his college roommates Andrew McCollum, Eduardo Saverin, Chris Hughes, and Dustin Moskovitz. It was launched on February 4, 2004, initially called "The Facebook" and was limited to Harvard University students. Later, it expanded to other universities and then opened to the general public in 2006.

Facebook's primary goal is to connect people globally, allowing users to create personal profiles, share updates, photos, videos, and engage with others through likes, comments, and private messages. Over the years, it has evolved into a comprehensive social networking site.

Key milestones in Facebook's history include:

2004: Founded at Harvard University.
2005: Expanded to universities outside Harvard and introduced photo-sharing features.
2006: Opened to everyone over the age of 13 with a valid email address and removed the "The" from its name, becoming just "Facebook."
2007: Introduced the Facebook Platform, enabling developers to build applications and games on the site.
2008: Introduced Facebook Chat, allowing real-time

messaging between users.

2010: Introduced the "Like" button and revamped the user interface.

2012: Acquired Instagram, a popular photo-sharing app, and reached one billion active users.

2014: Acquired WhatsApp, a messaging app with billions of users worldwide.

2015: Introduced Facebook Live, enabling live video streaming.

2016: Launched Reactions, expanding the range of emotional responses to posts beyond just "Like."

2018: Faced controversies regarding user data privacy and Cambridge Analytica.

2019: Announced plans for Libra, a cryptocurrency (later renamed Diem), which faced regulatory challenges.

2021: Mark Zuckerberg announced a company rebrand, changing the parent company's name to Meta Platforms Inc., emphasizing a focus on the metaverse.

Throughout its history, Facebook has faced scrutiny regarding privacy concerns, content moderation, and its influence on society. The platform has grown to be one of the largest and most influential social media networks globally, impacting how people communicate, share information, and connect with one another.

Google

Google was founded by Larry Page and Sergey Brin in September 1998 while they were pursuing their Ph.D. at Stanford University. Initially, the search engine was called "BackRub," but later it was renamed to "Google," inspired by the mathematical term "googol," which represents the number 1 followed by 100 zeros, signifying the vast amount of information they aimed to organize.

In 1996, Larry and Sergey developed the PageRank algorithm, which ranked web pages based on their relevance and popularity. This innovation significantly improved the accuracy of search results compared to other search engines at the time.

In 1998, they established Google Inc. as a private company, and their search engine quickly gained popularity due to its effectiveness and simplicity. Google's minimalist design, fast-loading pages, and accurate search results made it the go-to search engine for millions of users.

In 2000, Google launched its AdWords program, allowing businesses to display targeted ads based on users' search queries. This introduced a new revenue stream and played a significant role in the company's financial success.

Over the years, Google expanded its services to include Gmail, Google Maps, Google News, Google Images, and many other products that revolutionized how people accessed information and communicated online.

In 2004, Google went public, and its initial public offering (IPO) made Larry Page and Sergey Brin billionaires. The company's stock value continued to rise significantly, establishing Google as one of the world's most valuable technology companies.

In 2005, Google acquired Android Inc., laying the groundwork for the development of the Android operating system, which later became the dominant mobile OS worldwide.

In 2006, Google acquired YouTube, the popular video-sharing platform, further expanding its influence in the online space.

In 2008, Google introduced the Chrome web browser, which quickly gained popularity and became one of the most widely used browsers globally.

Throughout the years, Google's success continued to soar, with a series of acquisitions and innovations contributing to its expansion. It became a leader in cloud computing services with Google Cloud, and its parent company, Alphabet Inc., was formed in 2015 as part of a corporate restructuring.

Google's advertising platform, coupled with its diverse ecosystem of products and services, has allowed it to dominate the digital advertising market. Its search engine has remained the most popular worldwide, consistently holding a significant market share.

The success of Google can be attributed to its relentless focus on user experience, innovation, and the ability to adapt to changing technological landscapes.

Please note that this is a condensed history, and there are many more milestones and events that have contributed to Google's success.

AI

AI history is a captivating journey that spans decades. It all began in the 1950s when pioneers like Alan Turing and John McCarthy laid the foundation for the field. Early AI systems were built on rule-based logic and symbolic reasoning, but progress was slow due to limited computing power.

Over the years, AI evolved with breakthroughs like neural networks in the 1980s, which revived interest in the technology. However, it wasn't until the 21st century that AI truly flourished, thanks to advancements in machine learning, specifically deep learning. With the availability of vast data sets and powerful GPUs, AI applications started to excel in tasks like image recognition, natural language processing, and more.

The uses of AI have become incredibly diverse and impactful. In healthcare, AI assists in diagnosing diseases and designing personalized treatment plans. In transportation, it powers autonomous vehicles, improving road safety and efficiency. AI is also transforming industries like finance, marketing, and entertainment, enhancing decision-making and customer experiences.

Looking to the future, AI holds immense promise. It is expected to revolutionize various sectors, from education to agriculture. AI-driven education platforms can cater to individual learning styles, while smart farming techniques optimize crop yields and resource utilization. Additionally, AI's potential to tackle global challenges like climate change and resource management is being explored.

However, the future of AI also raises ethical and societal concerns. Ensuring responsible AI development, privacy protection, and avoiding bias are critical aspects that demand attention. Striking the right balance between innovation and ethical considerations will be vital in shaping a positive future for AI.

In conclusion, the history of AI showcases human ingenuity and perseverance. Its uses have transformed industries and improved lives, while its future promises even more exciting possibilities. As we navigate the AI landscape, let us embrace its potential responsibly, using it as a force for good, compassionately advancing our world into a brighter tomorrow.

Internet users of the world

As for writing a complete history about Internet usage, it's a vast topic that spans several decades, and it would be impractical to write a comprehensive history in this chat format. However, I can provide you with a condensed overview:

The Internet's origins can be traced back to the 1960s when the United States Department of Defense's Advanced Research Projects Agency (ARPA) developed the ARPANET. It was the first network to use the packet switching technique, laying the foundation for the modern Internet. ARPANET connected four universities, and by 1969, it facilitated the first message exchange between UCLA and Stanford.

In the 1970s, the TCP/IP protocol was developed, providing a standard for data transmission and allowing multiple networks to interconnect. This paved the way for the expansion of the Internet.

The 1980s saw the adoption of domain names and the development of the World Wide Web (WWW) by Tim Berners-Lee in 1989. The WWW introduced hyperlinks and allowed users to access information and navigate the internet with ease.

The 1990s marked a significant milestone with the commercialization of the Internet. Internet Service Providers (ISPs) emerged, making it accessible to the public. Popular web browsers like Netscape Navigator and Internet Explorer contributed to the Internet's rapid growth.

In the early 2000s, the dot-com bubble burst, but the Internet's usage continued to expand globally. Advancements in broadband technology and mobile devices further accelerated Internet adoption.

The rise of social media platforms in the mid-2000s, such as Facebook and Twitter, changed the way people interacted online. The widespread use of smartphones made the Internet more accessible to a broader population.

By the 2010s, the Internet became an integral part of daily life for billions of people worldwide. E-commerce, online education, streaming services, and cloud computing all contributed to its increasing prevalence.

To get the most accurate and up-to-date information about the current percentage of Internet users worldwide, I recommend referring to reliable sources or conducting a new search. As for submitting a complete history, it is beyond the scope of this chat, but you can explore various online resources and publications to delve deeper into this fascinating topic.

Send a message

The Dark Web

The dark web is a part of the internet that is not indexed by traditional search engines and can only be accessed through special software, such as the Tor browser. It is a subset of the deep web, which includes all web pages that are not indexed by search engines. The dark web operates on anonymous networks and is often associated with illicit activities due to its anonymity and lack of traceability.

The history of the dark web can be traced back to the 1970s and 1980s when researchers and military personnel were exploring ways to communicate securely and anonymously. The concept of onion routing, the technique behind the Tor network, was developed by the United States Naval Research Laboratory in the mid-1990s. The purpose was to protect sensitive government communications and allow individuals to browse the web without being tracked or monitored.

In 2002, the Tor project was officially launched as a free and open-source software, making it accessible to the public. It gained popularity over the years as it provided a way for individuals to protect their privacy and bypass internet censorship. However, the anonymity provided by the dark web also attracted various illegal activities.

The dark web is home to marketplaces where illegal goods and services are bought and sold, such as drugs, firearms, stolen data, and hacking tools. It has also become a platform for cybercriminals to exchange information and collaborate on various cyber attacks.

Beyond illegal activities, the dark web has also been used for legitimate purposes. It has served as a refuge for political dissidents, journalists, and activists in repressive regimes where internet censorship is prevalent. Tor has been a vital tool for whistleblowers and investigative journalists to communicate securely and anonymously with sources.

It's important to note that while the dark web is associated with illegal activities, it is not entirely a malicious place. There are legal and ethical reasons to use it, but caution and awareness are necessary due to its potential dangers and risks.

As the dark web continues to evolve, law enforcement agencies and governments worldwide have increased their efforts to combat illegal activities on these networks. They conduct investigations and operations to shut down illegal marketplaces and apprehend those engaged in criminal activities.

In conclusion, the dark web is a hidden part of the internet that offers anonymity and privacy but has also become a breeding ground for illegal activities. Its history is intertwined with the development of the Tor network, which was originally designed for secure communication and later became accessible to the public, leading to both positive and negative consequences for society.

Dark Web's worst form

The dark web, often associated with illicit activities, presents several concerning aspects:

Illegal marketplaces: The dark web hosts numerous illegal marketplaces where drugs, weapons, stolen data, and other illegal goods and services are bought and sold, enabling criminal activities.

Cybercrime: It serves as a hub for cybercriminals to share hacking tools, stolen data, and conduct activities like identity theft, credit card fraud, and distributed denial-of-service (DDoS) attacks.

Child exploitation: The dark web facilitates the distribution of explicit content involving minors, making it a platform for child exploitation and abuse.

Cyberattacks and malware: Malicious software, such as ransomware and trojans, can be purchased or exchanged on the dark web, leading to widespread cyberattacks and financial losses.

Privacy risks: While the dark web offers anonymity, it also attracts malicious actors who can exploit this feature to evade law enforcement and conduct criminal operations.

Terrorism and extremism: Extremist groups can use the dark web to communicate, recruit, and plan attacks away from the public eye.

Fraud and scams: Various scams, including phishing schemes and fake documents, are prevalent on the dark web, posing risks to unsuspecting individuals.

It's important to note that not all activities on the dark web are illegal, as it also hosts some legitimate and private platforms used for lawful purposes. However, the anonymity it provides can be abused, leading to significant challenges for law enforcement in combating cybercrime and other illicit activities.

Book description

"The Net Effect" is an insightful and captivating book that delves into the profound impact of the Internet on modern society. Through thought-provoking analysis and engaging anecdotes, the book explores how the digital revolution has transformed communication, commerce, and culture. From the rise of social media and online communities to the evolution of e-commerce and cybersecurity, the pages of "The Net Effect" offer a comprehensive exploration of the Internet's far-reaching influence on our lives. Whether you're a tech enthusiast, a business professional, or simply curious about the digital age, this book provides a compelling and informative journey into the fascinating world of the Internet and its effects on humanity.